THIS BOOK BELONGS TO

_____

_____

_____

KING*f*ISHER

THE FURTHER ADVENTURES OF
GOBBOLINO
AND THE LITTLE
WOODEN HORSE

THE COMPLETE COLLECTION

KINGFISHER CLASSICS

THE ADVENTURES OF TOM SAWYER
MARK TWAIN
ILLUSTRATED BY CLAIRE FLETCHER

BLACK BEAUTY
ANNA SEWELL
ILLUSTRATED BY IAN ANDREW

THE CALL OF THE WILD
JACK LONDON
ILLUSTRATED BY ANDREW DAVIDSON

HEIDI
JOHANNA SPYRI
ILLUSTRATED BY ANGELO RINALDI

THE SECRET GARDEN
FRANCES HODGSON BURNETT
ILLUSTRATED BY JASON COCKCROFT

TREASURE ISLAND
ROBERT LOUIS STEVENSON
ILLUSTRATED BY JOHN LAWRENCE

KINGFISHER MODERN CLASSICS

ADVENTURES OF THE LITTLE WOODEN HORSE
URSULA MORAY WILLIAMS
ILLUSTRATED BY PAUL HOWARD

THE FURTHER ADVENTURES OF GOBBOLINO AND THE LITTLE WOODEN HORSE
URSULA MORAY WILLIAMS
ILLUSTRATED BY PAUL HOWARD

GOBBOLINO THE WITCH'S CAT
URSULA MORAY WILLIAMS
ILLUSTRATED BY PAUL HOWARD

MILLY-MOLLY-MANDY STORIES
JOYCE LANKESTER BRISLEY
ILLUSTRATED BY JOYCE LANKESTER BRISLEY

TEDDY ROBINSON STORIES
JOAN G. ROBINSON
ILLUSTRATED BY JOAN G. ROBINSON

URSULA MORAY WILLIAMS

THE FURTHER ADVENTURES OF
GOBBOLINO
AND THE LITTLE
WOODEN HORSE

ILLUSTRATED BY
PAUL HOWARD

FOREWORD BY
PHILIPPA PEARCE

KING*f*ISHER

Publishers' Note:

The Publishers have used the first edition of *The Further Adventures of Gobbolino and the Little Wooden Horse*, published in Great Britain in 1984 by Puffin, for this publication. It is reproduced here complete and unabridged.

KINGFISHER
An imprint of Kingfisher Publications Plc
New Penderel House, 283-288 High Holborn, London WC1V 7HZ
www.kingfisherpub.com
a Houghton Mifflin Company imprint
215 Park Avenue South, New York, New York 10003
www.houghtonmifflinbooks.com

First published by Puffin in 1984
This edition published by Kingfisher 2002
(UK) 10 9 8 7 6 5 4 3 2 1
(US) 10 9 8 7 6 5 4 3 2 1

A CIP catalogue record for this book is available from the British Library.
LIBRARY OF CONGRESS CATALOGING-IN-PUBLICATION DATA has been applied for.

ISBN 0 7534 0714 0 (UK)
ISBN 0 7534 5495 5 (US)

Printed in India
1TR/0502/THOM/FR(MAR)/115INDWF(W)

For
ALEXANDRA

CONTENTS

FOREWORD

ALAS! I was born too early. In my own childhood I never knew *Adventures of the Little Wooden Horse* or *Gobbolino the Witch's Cat*. But both those heroes – each in his separate book – were there for my daughter when she was little. We loved them dearly, and followed their adventures with breathless attention.

Oddly, Gobbolino's great ambition since kittenhood was *not* to be a witch's cat (and, truly, he was no good at the black arts, anyway). He wanted only to be like other cats: an ordinary kitchen cat by a warm, friendly hearth, with a saucer of milk. But how difficult to achieve! Once, as a ship's cat at the very height of a storm whipped up by a sea witch, he refused just to save his own skin. Instead, he dared to counter-spell the witch ("Fiddlesticks to you, ma'am!") and so saved the ship and all its crew. But then the crew, in fear, turned against him and rejected him. He was homeless again. What little witchcraft he knew let him down.

Meanwhile, the little wooden horse was driven by a more straightforward ambition. Heroically, but without heroics, he resolved to earn enough money to save his dear creator and master, old Uncle Peder, from illness and penury. Like Gobbolino, and after as many hair-raising adventures, the little wooden horse achieved his particular ambition. Then he retired, so to speak. From Uncle Peder's cosy fireside he remarked, with typical modesty: "I am a quiet little horse, and for ever after I shall be rather a dull one."

How little does he foresee his future!

Like so many eager readers, my daughter and I would have liked sequels, one for each of our heroes. The years passed; none came. Then at last in 1984 – but at least in *very* good time for my grandchildren – came *The Further Adventures of Gobbolino and the Little Wooden Horse*. Here were those two familiar characters, those two old friends of ours from their two separate storybooks coming together in one brand-new story, in one book. A rarity in literature, I believe; and, in this instance, a treasure.

Reading this third book I do fuller justice to Gobbolino's qualities. He is still comfort-loving – that is cat nature. At the same time he is tender-hearted. He can respond – he finds that he *must* respond – to a difficult call on higher loyalty. One evening, after his milk in the farmhouse kitchen that is now his home, the little cat strolls out for a breath of fresh air before bed. A leaf has been dropped by a passing owl: "it stood out in the moonlight like a finger that beckoned". The leaf and the desperate message inscribed on it summon Gobbolino to the aid of his sister, Sootica, a thoroughgoing witch's cat, who still lives and works –

works mischief, of course – with her mistress in the faraway Hurricane Mountains.

With hardly a hesitation, Gobbolino leaves kitchen, milk and all other cat comforts. He will make for those sinister mountains, although the way there, he knows, will be long, dangerous and lonely.

Lonely? Then where does the little wooden horse come into this story?

Later on the very same morning that Gobbolino sets out, the little wooden horse trundles off into the forest to pick blackberries for Uncle Peder's wife, who will bottle them, and jam them, and bake them into pies. He is peacefully at work in a bramble-grown glade when . . . Who comes this way? A cat who is a stranger to him, a dark tabby with one white paw and rather surprising – and surprised – blue eyes.

And Gobbolino for the very first time sees a little wooden horse with green wheels, red saddle and blue stripes. "They greeted one another very civilly."

This all-important first meeting is low-key, like such classic first meetings as that of Holmes and Watson, or of Robin Hood and Little John. Yet note that, although the idea of the rescue mission is Gobbolino's, the little wooden horse is no mere sidekick. These two friends are equals, or rather, complementaries. A nearer approximation might be the first encounter of Ratty and Mole on the riverbank.

The enterprise to which our two heroes dedicate themselves leads to frightening adventures, and so the two of them – how like us! – are often frightened. But they never, ever give up. They are determined; they are resourceful. Above all, they both believe – they *know* – that they are doing the right thing, the good thing. The little wooden horse, for instance, is quite unused to the ways of witchcraft, but he always keeps a cool head, a clear vision. When he reproves the wayward and slippery Sootica, I seem again to hear the assured tones of my long-ago Headmistress at School Assembly.

I can reveal that the perilous undertaking of the two friends succeeds, against all odds – and in an unexpected way. Then they go home. And that's the end of their adventures; but not, of course, of them. Just imagine: "They had promised to meet one another at the very earliest opportunity. It might even be tomorrow! . . ."

Philippa Pearce

Great Shelford, 2002

1 A MESSAGE FOR GOBBOLINO

ONE EVENING IN LATE SUMMER, Gobbolino the kitchen cat was basking on the steps of his happy home, and thinking how lucky he was to have arrived in such agreeable surroundings after all the adventures that had befallen him as a witch's kitten.

"And I hardly deserve it," thought little Gobbolino, "for I was born and bred and brought up in the cavern of a witch. My little sister Sootica was happy enough learning to make wicked spells, and inventing naughty tricks to play on people. I wonder what has become of her now?"

He could hardly remember his mother, Grimalkin, but his sister had once been dear to his heart, and he could not help thinking of her now and again. True, she had teased and scoffed at him and called him all kinds of unkind names, but in the end she had saved his life when the witch wanted to get rid of him, and he hoped she had not suffered for it on his account.

While he lay drowsing in the sun the farm children were busy at their tasks on the farm. The girls were helping their mother in the dairy, making butter, skimming the cream and scalding the shining pans. The boys were working in the fields with their father, and presently everyone would come home to tea in the farmhouse, where nobody would pass him by without a kindly word or a chuck under the chin. It was a happy life for a kitchen cat, and Gobbolino expected it to last for ever.

Presently twilight fell, and the farmer's wife closed the dairy doors. She and her daughters, tired but contented, clattered across the yard to the kitchen, carrying jugs of cream and milk.

Down in the fields, gates were opening and shutting, horses' hooves were stamping, and the iron-rimmed wheels of the hay carts could be heard grinding across the stones of the farm lane. Now the finished hayricks would be standing like sentinels at the edge of the fields – food for the cattle in the long winter days to come. The farmer and his boys were trudging home to tea, content that life was mainly as it should be, and that the last of the hay was cut and stacked.

They stabled the horses and tramped into the house, stopping for a moment to say a friendly word to Gobbolino, who would only wait a very few minutes before he followed them into the kitchen. He knew there would be a saucer of milk set down for him at the fireside, and when it was finished he might choose any lap he liked to sit on, for the rest of the evening.

But as the rim of the sun dipped behind the far-off purple mountains, a large owl flew silently up the lane and dropped a leaf on the farmhouse steps, close to Gobbolino's feet.

In a minute the owl was gone, but the leaf flapped a little in the soft evening breeze, and came to rest by his paw. Even a moving shadow tempts a cat to chase it, so Gobbolino raised a forefoot and brought it down smartly on top of the leaf.

A flight of wild geese from the river below the

farm flew over his head, uttering their strange cries. Gobbolino ducked with his ears pressed close against his head, and when they were gone the leaf had fluttered halfway across the yard and was still flapping. Gobbolino got up to follow it, but voices called him from the kitchen door:

"Gobbolino! Gobbolino! It is supper-time and your milk is ready by the fire! Where are you, Gobbolino?"

Gobbolino trotted indoors.

His milk was warm and fresh as usual. The fire was hot and glowing. When the family had finished eating he waited until the farmer's wife sat down with her knitting, for the children were so restless he seldom got half an hour in peace upon their knees. While she cleared the table and washed the dishes he took a last, short stroll outside, and found that a great harvest moon had risen over the farmyard, making a new, white world of the barns and the straw stacks and the stables and the wagons quietly ranged beside the pond.

Halfway across the yard the leaf still lay, motionless

now, because the breeze had followed the sun behind the hills to rest.

Gobbolino walked across the yard and sniffed at the leaf, not so much from curiosity but because it stood out in the moonlight like a finger that beckoned, spoiling the lovely quiet carpet of light spread out in front of him.

As he lifted a paw to flatten the leaf against the earth, the moonlight shone upon a number of words written across the leaf, a sight that Gobbolino found exceptionally strange, since leaves fall off trees, and do not provide sheets of writing paper any more than trees provide writing tables in their native state. He held down the leaf with his forepaw and carefully read the inscription upon it.

When he had made out the meaning of the words written there he nearly fell over backwards in his astonishment, and for a moment his heart almost stopped beating. He raised his paw for the briefest second and the leaf fluttered away from him, stirred by the very last echo of the evening breeze. It disappeared underneath the chicken house.

Gobbolino found it after a while, among the shadows. Holding it very firmly this time he read aloud:

"PLEASE COME AND HELP ME, BROTHER! OH, PLEASE DO! OH, DO! DO!"

It was such an extraordinary message to be written on a leaf. And it was such an extraordinary message for a kitchen cat to receive! Gobbolino did not know what to make of it.

There was only one person in the world who had the right to call him brother, and that was his little sister Sootica, who was a witch's cat.

Long ago Gobbolino had been a witch's cat himself, until he was saved by a spell, and became what he had always longed to be, an ordinary kitchen cat with a home of his own and a coat that was almost tabby.

Nobody really liked witches' cats, or wanted them at their firesides. The farmer and his wife did not like them. Gobbolino remembered the day, now long ago, when they had turned him out into the wide world to fend for himself because he had blown sparks out

It was such an extraordinary message . . .

of his ears, and turned himself into all kinds of grotesque shapes and sizes to make the children laugh.

As he remembered those far-off days the old sensation of loneliness and not being wanted came back to him, and he shivered in the moonlight at the thought of his little sister Sootica feeling wretched and unhappy too, far up there in the Hurricane Mountains, or wherever else she might be now. And yet . . . his sister Sootica had been glad to be a witch's cat. Over and over again she had told him of her ambitions to know the book of magic by heart, to cast spells over people, and to fly down the night on a broomstick, making people cringe and shiver. She hoped to be the most famous witch's cat in all the world!

What could have happened to make her call for help in this manner? Was it possible that the witch had punished her with some dreadful revenge because she had rescued Gobbolino when he was about to be flung down the Hurricane Mountains? And because he owed her his life ought he not to help her when she called out to him?

But where could she be now? *Where?*

The owl never came back.

Gobbolino waited outside in the yard until the children came and chased him indoors.

"The hobgoblins will get you!" they teased him, spreading out his blanket beside the fire.

But all night long Sootica's message to him rang in his ears: "PLEASE COME AND HELP ME, BROTHER! OH, PLEASE DO! OH, DO! DO!"

2 THE LITTLE WOODEN HORSE

BY MORNING Gobbolino had not slept a wink all
night. He tried to tell himself that the message was
perhaps a trick to get him back into the witch's cave
and make him a slave again, but in his heart of hearts
he knew this was not true. Witches did not want
ordinary cats in their homes any more than ordinary
people wanted witches' cats, and she would be glad
to get rid of him.

Besides, there was something so beseeching, so
pleading in the message scrawled on the leaf that he
felt it could only have come from his sister Sootica.
And just as she had helped him before so he must
help her now.

It broke his heart to leave the farmhouse and the
kind family without a word of explanation, but he
was afraid that if he stopped to explain his mission

they would either prevent him from going, or, worse still, they would refuse to have him back again, because his sister was a witch, and with all his heart he counted on a welcome and his usual place by the fire when he came home.

He had made it his duty to watch the baby asleep in its basket under the apple trees, and again he was overcome with remorse at leaving his post. But one of the farm dogs, who was too old to go into the fields, kindly agreed to take his place, and just as the clock was striking seven in the morning Gobbolino crept out of the orchard, across the yard and away from the farm.

For the first mile he felt so lonely that half a dozen times he nearly turned back. It was so long since he had travelled all by himself. The happy bustle of the farmhouse, inside and out, had become so much a part of his new life that he did not realize how much he would miss it.

"But I shall soon be back again," Gobbolino comforted himself. "I don't know what I can do to help my sister, but once I see her I shall find out, and then I shall come home."

He set his face towards the Hurricane Mountains, because that was the only place he knew where his sister Sootica might be, and thinking, as he did, that every hour was bringing them closer together he began to feel much more cheerful, and even to purr a little as he trotted along.

"For I am such a lucky cat!" his heart sang. "I have a home to come back to, and kind friends to welcome me on my return. The children will be a little sad waiting for me and wondering when I am coming home, but when I do return they will be very happy, and everything will be as it was before."

The mountains were a great way off, and although Gobbolino walked all day they did not seem to come any nearer. He drank at a stream, but had had nothing to eat since leaving the farm, and his paws were so sore he could hardly stand up on them. Every now and again he stopped to give each of them a good lick, and to clean out the dust and grit from between his pads. This refreshed him a little, but he thought very anxiously about the next day and the next, and the terribly long distance he would have to walk before he reached the far-off Hurricane Mountains.

At last the road ran into a forest, and here the going was easier, because the pine needles made a carpet, quite springy and pleasant to walk upon.

Gobbolino was trotting along quite happily when he came upon a little wooden horse grazing in a small green glade.

They greeted one another very civilly. Gobbolino was delighted to find someone he could talk to for a little while, but he wished he were able to enjoy the berries that the little wooden horse was helping himself to from the bushes round the glade. Gobbolino noticed that he kept removing his head and putting them through the hole into his wooden body.

"Are those berries good to eat?" he asked the little wooden horse.

"Why yes! They are very good indeed!" said the little wooden horse. "But I am not picking them for myself. I am picking them for my mistress, the wife of my dear master, Uncle Peder the toy-maker, who lives close by, and she will turn them into jam, and put them into little pies, and bottle what is left over for the winter."

"Did you say you lived close by?" said Gobbolino eagerly. "Do you think your master has a shed where I could spend the night, and maybe catch a mouse or two for my supper? Because I still have a long way to go," he added, "and I have had nothing to eat all day."

"Why! You must come home with me at once!" said the little wooden horse. "My missus will give you something nice to eat and a comfortable bed for the night. Follow me!"

He set out at such a pace on his twinkling wooden legs, with his wooden wheels spinning round like tops, that Gobbolino could only limp after him, losing distance all the way.

When the little wooden horse saw how he was faltering he came cantering back and exclaimed in sympathy:

"Why! You are quite lame! You must have blisters on all four of your feet! Jump on my back, and I will take you to my home!"

Gobbolino was only too grateful to jump on to the wooden back of his kind friend. He saw how strong was the little wooden horse, and how well made.

His stripes were blue and freshly painted. His saddle was red and his spots were black, yet there was nothing brand-new about him. He seemed wise and good and kind, as if he had been around some time in the world, and Gobbolino wondered very much how he came to be in this wood, and what was his story.

But before he could ask him any questions they arrived at a little house in the middle of the forest. It was built with white walls, a green painted door, and there was a pretty dovecot in the garden.

The little wooden horse trotted through the garden gate and deposited Gobbolino at the door, which he then pushed open with his wooden wheels, and led the cat inside.

A rosy-faced old woman was cooking at the kitchen stove, and from her cooking came the most delicious flavoursome smells.

Gobbolino had not intended to go into the house. He meant to find a corner where he could spend the night in the garden. But the little wooden horse was blocking the doorway, and before he could escape the old woman had turned round.

"Well, I never!" she exclaimed in surprise. "Whatever have we got here now? What a handsome cat! What lovely dark fur, and what beautiful blue eyes! Wherever did you find him?"

The little wooden horse was explaining how they had come across each other while picking blackberries in the forest, but at that moment the door behind them gave way to a tall, handsome old man who at once took the little wooden horse's head in his hands and began to rub it very affectionately.

Before many minutes had passed Gobbolino found himself lapping a saucer of rich yellow milk, while a comfortable cushion awaited his tired feet. Kind hands brushed and combed his fur and, while the old woman disposed of the berries the little wooden horse had picked in the glade, Gobbolino fell fast asleep, lulled by the bubbling of the pot and the crackling of the fire.

He slept so soundly that he did not wake up all night. When he opened his eyes it was morning, and there was nobody in the kitchen but himself and the little old woman.

She was just as kind to him as she had been the night before, and, when he went into the garden to find his friend the little wooden horse, she explained to him that the horse had gone off with his master, Uncle Peder, to take some toys to a far-off customer, and they would not be home until nightfall.

Gobbolino was very disappointed, for he wanted to say goodbye and to thank the little wooden horse before he went on his journey, but he knew he ought to leave early if he was to get well on his way to the Hurricane Mountains before dark.

He explained this to the old woman, who looked disappointed in her turn.

"I thought you were coming to live with us!" she said reproachfully. "Why are you in such a hurry to get to the Hurricane Mountains?"

Gobbolino began to tell her his story.

"I have a good home of my own to return to," he explained, "but I have a little sister high up in the mountains, who belongs to a witch. I am afraid she may be in some kind of trouble, because she sent me a message to come and help her, and that is where

I am going. I am truly grateful, ma'am, for your hospitality, and I so badly wanted to say goodbye to my friend the little wooden horse before I left."

But the old woman was looking at him with horror in her face.

"Your sister is a *witch's* cat?" she exclaimed. "Then what are you?"

"I am a kitchen cat!" said Gobbolino simply, but she turned away and began to make such a clatter with the pots and pans that he felt sure she did not believe him. He crept into a corner of the kitchen and tears of shame filled his beautiful blue eyes. He was afraid that if he left the house now his friend the wooden horse would get into trouble for bringing a witch's cat into the house. Twice he left the kitchen and trotted out through the garden gate, but twice he came back again. His paws, too, were so sore he realized he would not be able to go far without another day's rest, so he crept into a little potting shed in the garden and waited until he could tell the whole of his story to the little wooden horse.

Late in the afternoon Uncle Peder and the wooden

horse returned. Gobbolino was about to run out and greet them, but he saw the old woman in the doorway, and he did not want to run the risk of being sent away without an explanation.

So he crouched in the shed, and heard his wooden friend inquiring anxiously where the cat was, and whether his paws had healed during the day.

"Why, I have no idea where your friend the cat is," said the old woman testily. "I haven't seen it since breakfast-time this morning. And a fine trick you played on me!" she added, rounding on the little wooden horse. "It is just a bold, wicked witch's cat, off to join its sister witch in the Hurricane Mountains! We don't want that sort of thing here!"

"I can't believe such a story!" said Uncle Peder in astonishment. "That was a *good* cat if ever I saw one! Remember, wife, you made a mistake once before, and it is quite possible to make one again!"

"Oh dear! Oh dear! How hasty I am!" lamented the old woman, remembering the time, long ago, when she had chased away the little wooden horse from her door. "Well you may be right, Uncle Peder, and I am wrong . . . but the creature told me himself that his sister was a witch's cat, and what does that make him himself I should like to know?"

Gobbolino stole out of the potting shed and into the kitchen. He sat down beside the little wooden horse and told his whole story to the family.

The old woman was ashamed that she had not listened to him before. She gave him an excellent dinner, and began to put scraps of food into a little bag for him on his journey to the mountains.

"I must set off immediately," Gobbolino said in some anxiety, "because I have wasted a whole day, and my sister must be desperate to know if I am coming."

"You can't go into the forest by night!" the little wooden horse said. "It is very dangerous, and you could lose your way. Wait until first light in the morning, and then I will go with you as far as the open plain, and see you on your journey."

Having heard his story Uncle Peder and the old woman were quite agreed that the little wooden horse should go a short way with him and see him on his journey, especially since Gobbolino's paws were

He . . . told his whole story to the family.

by no means healed, and he had many miles to travel before he came to the Hurricane Mountains.

"But come back to us as soon as you have seen your friend on his way!" they told the little wooden horse. "Because if anything happened to you it would break our hearts. We could not possibly go on living without you now!"

Gobbolino and the little wooden horse lay down together beside the fire and slept till early dawn. Then they each took a bag of food that the old woman had prepared for them and set out into the forest, with the early morning awakening all around them, bird calls, spiders' threads, little gold dawn clouds in the sky above, and mists weaving and waving between the distant trees.

Gobbolino hopped along on his healing feet, using three paws at a time to rest the other, until the wooden horse persuaded him to ride while he could, and save himself for the rougher roads when he would have no one to help him.

3 THE OWL

SEVERAL TIMES during the day Gobbolino begged the little wooden horse to set him down and go back to Uncle Peder and his wife, but the horse only said:

"Wait a little! Only just a little while longer and we shall have come to the end of the forest. I will go home then."

At last it seemed that the trees were thinning out, and the dense woods were coming to an end.

But the light that was filtering through the branches was less bright, because the sun had gone behind the clouds, and it became quite obvious that a large storm was blowing up in the sky.

"Now isn't that tiresome!" said the little wooden horse. "While we were deep inside the forest it couldn't have harmed us very much, but now that the trees are thinner there is no shelter and nowhere to hide ourselves. We shall just have to make up our minds to get soaking wet until the storm is over."

Beyond the trees the landscape spread far out across meadows and valleys, and still infinitely distant appeared the ramparts of the Hurricane Mountains, now shrouded in a pall of driving rain.

"I thought we must be nearly there!" said Gobbolino sorrowfully. "They look every bit as far away as when I first left home. And just suppose, when I arrive there, I find my sister is not there at all? Whatever shall I do?"

They both realized that besides the rain, night was now falling, and as the darkness slowly enveloped them they could not tell if it were stormclouds or evening that was stealing the daylight out of the sky.

The rainclouds dallied over the meadows, but a few heavy drops spattered Gobbolino and the little wooden horse huddling together under a tree.

Suddenly Gobbolino became aware of a large owl sitting above them on a branch, looking at them very seriously out of round amber eyes, which it closed the moment they looked back at it.

Remembering the owl who had brought him his sister's message he stood on his hind legs with his paws reaching up the bole of the tree, while he begged the owl to tell him if he really were the same bird or quite a different one.

The owl took absolutely no notice of him. If anything it closed its eyes rather tighter than before.

It must be quite another owl, Gobbolino thought, but on the other hand, owls flew far and wide, and knew a great deal about the goings-on in field and forest, and in the district round them.

"Sir Owl!" Gobbolino called politely. "Please can you tell me one thing? Do you know whether a witch still lives in the Hurricane Mountains, in a cavern right at the top?"

The owl's great amber eyes opened wide for a moment, and then shut up tightly, like boxes.

"Oh, please, please tell me, Sir Owl," Gobbolino pleaded. "It is so very important to me to know if there is a cavern up there still lived in by a witch! Please tell me if you can! Please do!"

The owl gave the faintest nod of its head, although its eyes remained tightly closed.

"And does the witch have a cat?" asked Gobbolino, trembling with excitement.

This time the owl's nod was so faint that he looked down at the wooden horse in perplexity.

"It said 'yes'!" said the little wooden horse quite positively. "But I think you forgot to say 'Thank you!'"

"Oh, thank you! Thank you, kind Owl!" said Gobbolino, much abashed. "And please, sir, please will you tell me . . . does the cat have a name? And can you tell me if that name could be Sootica?"

At that, the owl gave such a loud screech that both the friends were startled. Gobbolino fell backwards from the tree, and at the same moment the owl left the branch above and sailed away into the darkness.

The single drops of rain became a downpour that battered the scanty branches and fell upon their heads like wet pebbles. The little wooden horse turned his head towards the tree and told Gobbolino to crouch underneath his wooden body,

"... does the cat have a name?"

but there was not much protection there. In his turn Gobbolino tried to shroud the little wooden horse in his fur.

"How ashamed I am at bringing you so far from your home!" Gobbolino said. "You could be warm and comfortable beside your own kitchen fire if you had not chosen to come and help me find my little sister. First thing in the morning you must go home, for I can see my way now as far as the mountains, and when the storm is over and the daylight comes I can find the road to them alone."

"We will see about that," said the little wooden horse, "but just remember, I came of my own accord. You have nothing to feel ashamed about."

It became so dark that they could no longer see each other, but Gobbolino knew his friend was there by the feel of his strong and sturdy legs, and the four wooden wheels at the ends of them, while the little wooden horse could feel Gobbolino's soft coat until the rain turned it into a soaking wet blanket that dripped wet on to the earth around them.

Above them the storm roared and raged till they

seemed surrounded by clamour and the relentless sweep of the drenching rain.

Suddenly the noise became much fainter, and then ceased. At the same time something like a thick, soft eiderdown descended gently on top of them, wrapping them closely and blotting out the sound of the storm. Their cold wet bodies began to glow with warmth and dry themselves, their feet felt warm and cosy, and they sank gratefully into the soft feathers of the owl's wings spread over the pair of them, to dry and comfort them during the night.

4 THE CHASE

THEY AWOKE TO BRIGHT SUNLIGHT. The owl was gone, leaving them warm and dry.

Gobbolino's fur shone like silk, while the paint on the little wooden horse gleamed as if it had just been polished.

The Hurricane Mountains were clean and blue in the morning light. They did not look so far away after all.

"Why! I shall get there by the evening!" said Gobbolino joyously. "Now you can go home again, my kind friend, because I really cannot accept your kindness any longer. You can be quite certain that by this time tomorrow I will have found my little sister Sootica!"

The little wooden horse looked doubtful.

"And what then?" he said. "After such a long journey you will be much too tired to confront the witch or any other danger that may threaten her. While I am beside you, you can ride on my back and keep your strength for any adventures still to come. I will go just a little further with you before I turn back."

Gobbolino could only be grateful, as much for his company as for his help and kindness. His paws were nearly healed, and since there was no sign of the owl, they left the forest and stepped out across the vast plateau of fields and meadows towards the mountains.

They were very glad of the food that the old woman had given them for their journey, and they had eaten their dinner beside a little stream in the middle of the plain when Gobbolino raised his head and exclaimed, "What is that strange noise I can hear?"

The little wooden horse listened too, but the noise had died away, and they finished their meal.

Gobbolino heard it again.

"There! Far away to the west of us! It sounds like wild birds crying, only different . . . quite different! Don't you hear it yourself?"

The little wooden horse did hear it. He raised his wooden head and sniffed the air.

"I can hear it!" he said. "And I think we ought to go back to the forest as quickly as we can!"

"*What?*" exclaimed Gobbolino in horror. "When we have come so far? Just look what a long way behind us the trees are! Why! We are more than halfway to the mountains already! Don't let's go back! Let's go on as quickly as we can!"

The sound had ceased. The little wooden horse jumped to his feet and stood looking westward with his ears pricked.

"I think we should go back to the forest!" he repeated solemnly.

Gobbolino looked at him in astonishment.

"What are you afraid of?" he asked. "How can wild birds hurt us . . . if it is wild birds?"

"Supposing it isn't wild birds!" said the little wooden horse. "Supposing it is . . . wild . . . things!"

"Not wild beasts?" said Gobbolino. "How could it possibly be? Not lions! Not tigers nor hyenas! Not leopards! And wolves hunt in the forests, yet you want us to go back there!"

"Dogs!" said the little wooden horse flatly.

"Dogs?" screeched Gobbolino jumping three feet into the air.

"Hounds . . . ! On the scent . . ." said the little wooden horse. "I don't know what scent . . . but if they smell us it could be us. Jump on my back and see if you can tell me which way they are coming."

Gobbolino jumped on to the back of the little wooden horse, standing up as high on his hind legs as he could stretch himself. But far as he could view across the western plain there was nothing threatening in the landscape, and the noise of the baying had quite died away and disappeared.

"I daresay they are not coming in this direction after all!" said the little wooden horse, much relieved.

"Then we can go on!" said Gobbolino happily.

"I still think we should go back and wait till evening," said the little wooden horse. "By then the hounds will have gone home, and we can travel quite easily out in the open. There will be some moonlight presently to help us."

"But we shall have lost so much time!" wailed Gobbolino. "We ought to be in the mountains by sundown, and if we go back we won't be there till late tomorrow. Let's wait a little while and listen, and if they come no nearer we can go on our way!"

Together they crouched down by the stream where they had eaten their dinner, listening to every sound that came across the plain – the trilling of the larks above, the sizzling of the crickets, the babble of the water and the spasmodic chirp of a water bird. There was no other sound at all.

"We must go on!" said Gobbolino. "Every minute is important if I am to reach the mountains before the sun sets."

The little wooden horse still hesitated.

"This is where we must part, my kind little friend!" said Gobbolino. "I will go on to the mountains and you must go home. We will both be well on our separate journeys before dark. I have so much to thank you for, and I cannot accept any more of your kindness or your companionship. It is time that we said goodbye."

The little wooden horse looked very unhappy, shifting from one wooden leg to the other.

"I would gladly go further with you," he said at last,

"but I have such a very strong feeling that we ought both to go back to the forest and wait till evening."

"I can't see any reason for it!" said Gobbolino pettishly. "All those miles backwards when we could be going forwards? How can you think of such a thing? Go back by all means, my dear faithful friend, but don't ask me to come too until I have found my sister and heard what she wants of me. How can you possibly think of asking me to turn my back on the mountains now?"

The little wooden horse began to paw the ground in an agony of embarrassment and distress. When he saw that nothing he said would move Gobbolino he bowed his wooden head and said very sadly:

"Very well, my friend, we will do as you say! I will go home to my dear old master and missus, who need me even more than you do, and I will wish you the very best of luck on your journey, and protection from every danger. For I am very much afraid there *will* be danger!" the little wooden horse said sadly, but Gobbolino only tossed his head, while a spark of bravado flashed in his beautiful blue eyes as he exclaimed, "Danger? Why! Haven't I met danger before? Haven't I confronted witches and spells and wicked enchantments, and been flown away with on a broomstick and dropped in a raging river? Do you think I am afraid of danger, my little wooden friend? Not I!"

But the little wooden horse was looking forwards across the plain, not north to the Hurricane Mountains. His wooden ears were pricked and listening, although no sound came but the flutter of the wind in the grass, the trilling of the larks, the sizzling of the crickets, the babble of the water, and now and again the sudden chirp downstream of a water bird.

"Goodbye, Gobbolino!" he said quietly. "May your journey be successful, and I hope you will soon find your sister. I shall watch every day for your return once you have helped her. Be sure you come by the cottage on your journey home, and tell us all your adventures. Goodbye!"

There were tears in the eyes of the little wooden horse, and Gobbolino was crying too. He thanked his friend over and over again for his companionship, assuring him that he would never have come as far as this if he had not had his help, and been able to rest his blistered paws by riding on the horse's back.

Very sadly they climbed up opposite sides of the stream, and set off, one northwards to the mountains, and the other southwards to the forest and home. Every now and again they turned and waved to one another until the tall grasses enveloped them, and the great vast plain seemed as empty as if it had swallowed up the pair of them.

Gobbolino felt terribly lonely, but nothing would have persuaded him to retrace his footsteps, and with every pace forward he congratulated himself on getting nearer and nearer to his goal.

"How could I possibly have gone back to the forest?" he asked himself. "My sister will be counting the minutes till I arrive, and already she will be wondering why I have not come sooner!"

He had trotted on for more than an hour, and had made a wide circle to avoid one of the few farms and villages that were dotted about the plain, when he heard again the strange sound that had so disturbed the senses of the little wooden horse.

From the far westward came the cry of hounds moving up the plain, a long protracted baying that could no longer be confused with the cry of geese, or of any other bird. It was unmistakably the baying of a pack of hounds.

Gobbolino's heart began to thump. At the same time he quickened his pace, hurrying along on his four paws that were once more sore and aching. The noise was a great distance off, and no doubt the hounds were after their own quarry, and had nothing to do with him at all, but they were closer than they had been when the two friends ate their dinner beside the stream, and it was quite possible that they were coming back to their kennels in the village and might cross his trail.

Gobbolino began to gallop, the little bag of food bouncing up and down under his chin. It became such a burden that he threw it away, and was able to run faster without it, but the baying of the hounds came nearer.

The pack was sweeping up the plain now, and Gobbolino realized at last the honest fears of the little wooden horse, for there was not a rock, not a tree where he could hide himself until they passed. He turned his face towards the village, hoping he might reach it in time to find a shed or a shelter of some kind before the hounds overtook him. He tried not to think of other dangers like watchdogs or youths with sticks, or stones being thrown at him, or similar dangers. The threat behind him was quite enough to concentrate on while he was running.

He galloped along gasping with terror, and now it seemed almost certain that the hounds had found his trail, for the baying grew louder and louder and more terrifying the faster he ran.

And another sound had joined them – a rattling, clattering noise that pursued him and came closer and closer, with snorts and blowings and the thunder of spinning wooden wheels.

Gobbolino was about to fall flat on his face from sheer terror when a familiar voice panted in his ear, "Jump on my back, Gobbolino! Don't stop for a moment! Jump, I tell you! Jump!"

"Jump on my back, Gobbolino!"

The little wooden horse overtook him at full gallop, and with a desperate leap Gobbolino gained the painted saddle and they tore on, clinging together as the horse's wooden wheels spun and clattered across the plain.

The hounds were not far behind them, and the baying was terrible. It was quite obvious that they had picked up Gobbolino's scent and were following it in full cry.

But all of a sudden the baying died down, as if the pack had stopped for a moment, or overrun the trail. They seemed to be casting about to find it again, uttering little whimpers and false cries before returning to the same place again, and once more becoming bewildered and more and more defeated. This happened at the point where Gobbolino jumped on to the back of the little wooden horse, and his scent gave place to the trail of wooden wheels. For a short time it seemed as if the two friends had escaped from their pursuers.

Then the hounds realized that the scent they were following was mingled with the smell of wood and paint. It was still there, though faint and uncertain. All they had to do was to follow the new smell of paint and wood, and with a united howl of delight they set off again.

Now, although the little wooden horse sped like a streak of lightning, the hounds were gaining on him fast.

"Put me down and let me run!" Gobbolino pleaded, for he felt sure his weight was holding back the speed of the little wooden horse, but even side by side they could not outpace the pack of hounds.

When both were at the end of their strength and about to turn and face the baying pack, they arrived suddenly at the gate of an ancient church, and slipping quickly through the lych-gate, arrived inside the churchyard.

5 SANCTUARY IN THE HAUNTED CHURCH

AN OLD PRIEST came from the doorway of the church and walked down the path of the churchyard.

Gobbolino and the little wooden horse flew to hide themselves in the folds of his cassock, as a last and desperate refuge from the hounds, but to their amazement the pack stopped short at the lych-gate. One or two jumped over the wall and ran about among the tombstones, but they seemed very uneasy, and took no further notice of their prey.

The next moment a fearful clanging of bells in every discord burst out of the belfry above their heads. The old priest flinched, closed his eyes and crossed himself. A crowd of terrified bats flew out of the tower, and every hound turned tail and fled, howling. They could be heard retreating, still

A crowd of terrified bats flew out of the tower . . .

howling, across the plain, until they had run quite out of earshot.

The old priest stooped down, and gently stroking Gobbolino murmured:

"Ah, my little cat! For once the haunted church has stood you in good stead, for I think it has saved your life!"

While they had been running for their lives the first shades of evening had crept across the plain, and were mingling with the pink glow on the peaks of the Hurricane Mountains.

At first Gobbolino and the little wooden horse were too shaken and breathless to tell their story to the priest, but as they recovered their breath they asked him if they might have sanctuary in the church overnight.

"Sanctuary!" exclaimed the priest. "Yes, of course you may have sanctuary! But I doubt if any of my parishioners would call it that! The church is haunted. You heard for yourselves the terrible clamour of the bells, though nobody rings them! The bell-ringers refuse to come any more. The choir won't

AUTHOR NOTE

WHEN URSULA MORAY WILLIAMS was a little girl, she and her twin sister Barbara were sent to bed so early that they used to tell each other stories to pass the time before they went to sleep. After their mother had taught them to read and write, they began to make books – writing new stories and illustrating them with coloured pictures – which they gave to each other at Christmas or on their birthday. They made these "anniversary books" every year until they were teenagers. When they grew up, Ursula became a writer and Barbara a painter, and they remained close – although Ursula lived in England and her sister in Iceland.

Their parents, who were at one time both teachers, gave the girls and their younger brother the happiest of childhoods. The house where they lived was a huge old mansion lit by oil lamps, with an entrance hall paved in marble and surrounded by glass cases full of stuffed birds and animals – foxes, owls, weasels, jays and a large golden pheasant. The house was crumbling, and Ursula remembers that for their lessons with a governess "we moved from room to room as the ceilings fell on us." But it was a wonderful place to play in (there was a church organ that had no keyboard but provided a perfect hiding-place) – and in the big park outside they had a much-loved pony and cart.

In 1928, when the twins were nearly seventeen (they were born on 19th April 1911), they were sent to France for a year to live in a pastor's house in Annecy in the Alps. There they had to go to school – which they hated – but out of school they enjoyed every moment: swimming, climbing, skiing and picnicking in the beautiful countryside. Ursula describes this time as like living in a fairy tale. When they came home, both sisters enrolled at the Winchester College of Art, but, while Barbara thrived, Ursula dropped out after a year and decided to practise her writing at home. She was encouraged by her uncle, Stanley Unwin (who was the famous publisher of *The Hobbit*), and her first book, *Jean-Pierre*, a story set in the mountains of Annecy, was published in 1931 with her own illustrations. She remembers that the book cost just 2s 6d (12½ pence)!

In 1935 Ursula married Conrad Southey John (always called Peter after their marriage), the great-grandson of the poet Robert Southey. To him she dedicated her best-known story, *Adventures of the Little Wooden Horse*, written when she was expecting their first child, Andrew. Three more sons followed – Hugh, Robin and Jamie. The four boys were taken out in the afternoons, allowing Ursula to concentrate on her writing for two hours a day, and it was during this time that she created *Gobbolino the Witch's Cat* (1942). It was over forty years later that Ursula's two most endearing characters came together in one book, *The Further Adventures of Gobbolino and the Little Wooden Horse* (1984).

Ursula has written over seventy books for children. "I write compulsively," she says. "During the war years I was cooking for ten of us but I *had* to write, just as my twin sister had to paint and design." Her husband died in 1974, but she still lives in the family farmhouse on Bredon Hill in Gloucestershire where she brought up her children so happily. Ursula has ten grandchildren and many great-grandchildren.